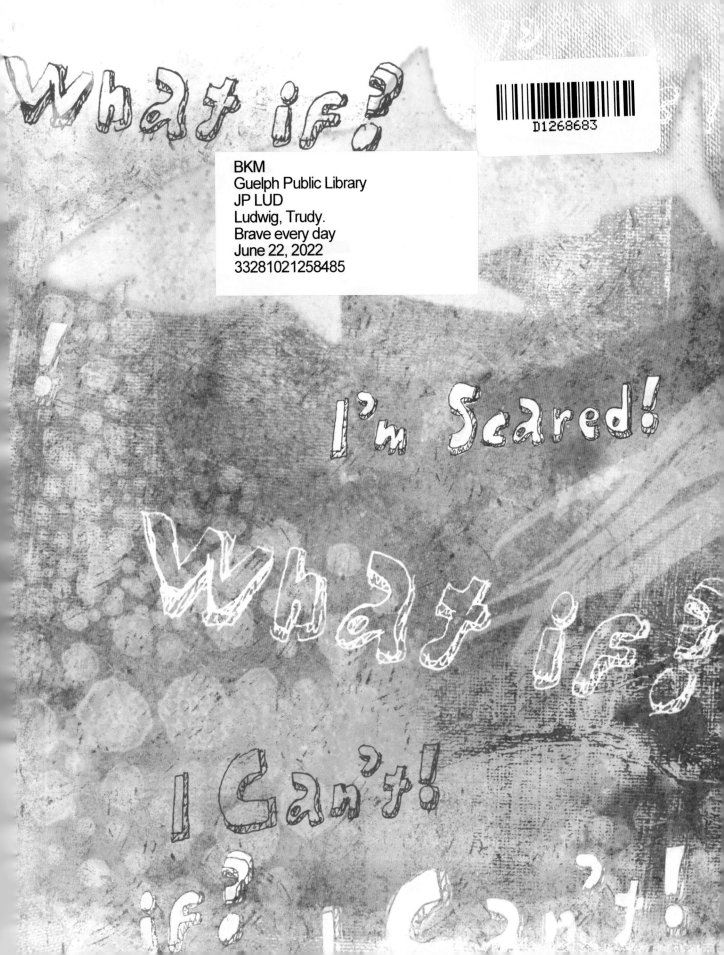

What if?

I'm Scared!

What if?

I Can't!

if? I Can't!

BRAVE
EVERY
DAY

by
Trudy Ludwig

illustrated by
Patrice Barton

Alfred A. Knopf
New York

Most kids love hide-and-seek.

Not Camila. She just wants to hide.

Hiding is what Camila does
best when she worries.

And she worries a lot.

Every morning, Camila's **What if** worries show up uninvited and follow her out the door.

What if the bus doesn't show up?

What if Mrs. Flores calls on me and I don't know the answer?

What if I have no one to play with at recess?

Her **I can't** worries sneak up on her at school.

I can't go first.

I can't read this aloud with everyone looking at me.

I can't take this test without my favorite eraser!

And her **I'm scared** worries visit her at night.

Camila doesn't think of herself
as very brave, but she is.
She just doesn't know it yet.

One Monday morning, Mrs. Flores has exciting news to share: "We'll be going to the aquarium next week!"

Bubbling with excitement, many students rush
to pick up the forms. Not Camila. Her worries keep
her firmly anchored to her seat.

"Have you ever been to an aquarium?"
asks Mrs. Flores.

"No," squeaks Camila.
"Well, I'm sure you'll enjoy the field trip."
But Camila isn't so sure.

"What's the matter, Camila—afraid you'll get eaten by a big ol' hungry shark?" taunts Wyatt. "Or inked by an octopus?" teases Remi.

Camila sinks lower in her seat as her worries weigh her down.

"That's enough, you two," warns Mrs. Flores as she moves on to Kai's desk.

For the rest of the week, Camila worries about all the things that could go wrong at the aquarium.

When the big day arrives, Camila tries her best to blend into the background, avoiding crowds of kids and scary sea creatures.

Feeling overwhelmed,
Camila finds a hiding spot
to catch her breath—

only to discover Kai
already there!

"Are you okay?" asks Camila.

"Not really," says Kai. "This is my one big chance to be right next to a real, live stingray, and now I'm scared to do it."

"But I thought you loved this kind of stuff."

"Well, I love *reading* about it . . . ," says Kai. "Maybe it would help if we both go in there together. What do you think?"

"Umm . . . ," says Camila as she struggles to get her words out. "I . . . ahhh . . ."

"Will you please, *pleeeease* come with me?"

Seeing Kai so nervous makes Camila realize her heart is bigger than her fears. Instead of *What If, I Can't,* and *I'm Scared,* Camila says . . .

Now, whenever Camila feels the need to hide,
she bravely keeps on trying—in both big and little
ways—to make sure that she gets found.

Ready or not, here I come!

For all the worriers who go beyond
their comfort zone every single day:
You are true warriors in my book!
—T.L.

For all those who are brave
but just don't know it yet.
—P.B.

THIS IS A BORZOI BOOK PUBLISHED BY ALFRED A. KNOPF

Text copyright © 2022 by Trudy Ludwig
Jacket art and interior illustrations copyright © 2022 by Patrice Barton
All rights reserved. Published in the United States by Alfred A. Knopf, an imprint of
Random House Children's Books, a division of Penguin Random House LLC, New York.
Knopf, Borzoi Books, and the colophon are registered trademarks of Penguin Random House LLC.

Visit us on the Web! rhcbooks.com
Educators and librarians, for a variety of teaching tools, visit us at RHTeachersLibrarians.com

Library of Congress Cataloging-in-Publication Data is available upon request.
ISBN 978-0-593-30637-6 (hardcover) — ISBN 978-0-593-30638-3 (library binding) — ISBN 978-0-593-30639-0 (ebook)
The text of this book is set in 17-point Meta Pro. The illustrations were created using pencil sketches, digitally painted.
Interior design by Sarah Hokanson
MANUFACTURED IN CHINA   June 2022   10 9 8 7 6 5 4 3 2 1   First Edition
Random House Children's Books supports the First Amendment and celebrates the right to read.

QUESTIONS FOR DISCUSSION

Most kids love hide-and-seek. Not Camila. She just wants to hide.

- Why does Camila want to hide?
- What are the three types of worries Camila deals with every day?
- Have you ever experienced these kinds of worries? If yes, which ones?

"What's the matter, Camila—afraid you'll get eaten by a big ol' hungry shark?" taunts Wyatt. "Or inked by an octopus?" teases Remi.

- Why do you think Camila isn't as excited as the other kids about going to the aquarium?
- How do you think it makes Camila feel when Wyatt and Remi make fun of her worries?
- What could Wyatt and Remi have said or done instead to make Camila feel better?

Seeing Kai so nervous makes Camila realize her heart is bigger than her fears.

- What does it mean to be brave?
- Do you think it's possible to be brave *and* scared at the same time? Explain why or why not.
- Why do you think the author chose the title *Brave Every Day* for this story?

Instead of What if?, I can't!, *and* I'm scared!, *Camila says* . . . *"I'll try!"*

- It can be scary trying something new. Give an example of something you were scared to try that turned out better than expected.
- How can you help someone who is scared to try something new?
- What can you do to feel calmer when you're scared, anxious, or worried?

RECOMMENDED READING FOR KIDS

Alber, Diane. *A Little Spot of Anxiety: A Story About Calming Your Worries.* Mesa, AZ: Diane Alber Art LLC, 2020.

Henkes, Kevin. *Wemberly Worried.* New York: Greenwillow Books, 2010.

Huebner, Dawn, PhD. Dr. Dawn's Mini Books About Mighty Fears series. Philadelphia: Jessica Kingsley Publishers, 2022.

Huebner, Dawn, PhD, and Bonnie Matthews (illustrator). *What to Do When You Worry Too Much: A Kid's Guide to Overcoming Anxiety.* Washington, DC: Magination Press, 2006.

Percival, Tom. *Ruby Finds a Worry.* New York: Bloomsbury Children's Books, 2019.

Santat, Dan. *After the Fall: How Humpty Dumpty Got Back Up Again.* New York: Roaring Brook Press, 2017.

Telgemeier, Raina. *Guts.* New York: Scholastic, 2019.

Zuppardi, Sam. *Jack's Worry.* Somerville, MA: Candlewick Press, 2016.